Amadeus

The Leghorn Rooster

For Cameron + William

story by

Delores B. Nevils

Delores B Nevils

illustrations by

Jonathan Green

Jonathan Green

SANDLAPPER PUBLISHING CO., INC.
ORANGEBURG, SOUTH CAROLINA 29115

On the island of St. Helena, there is a widow lady who lives in a tiny cottage that has twenty-six windows. A ramp, painted red, leads to the doorway.

Clusters of pink and red azaleas and yellow forsythia line the circular drive. In the springtime, the widow lady's yard is a wonderland of pretty colors.

Palmetto trees, South Carolina's state tree, surround the cottage. From the many windows, Widow Lady watches the tall palmettos bow and sway, bow and sway when strong winds blow in from the Atlantic Ocean. The trees wave to passers-by, inviting them to come into the tiny cottage for a visit.

Two kittens, a mother cat, and two dogs came to live with the widow lady.

Scooter was a gray and white kitten. Pumpkin was white and orange—the color is how she got her name. Mae Liza, the mama cat, was gray striped with four white paws that looked like little shoes.

The cats did not live in the tiny cottage. They lived outside where they could run and play. When the weather turned cold, they scampered under the house and burrowed in leaves the wind blew there. Snuggled together, they kept cozy and warm.

Whenever the widow lady was in her yard, Mae Liza walked close to her, purring and purring. The mother cat knew Scooter and Pumpkin loved the widow lady very much.

The dogs were named Kane and Able. Kane was golden brown with white spots on his neck and ears. He was big, weighing about a hundred pounds. Able was Kane's brother. He was smaller, but his fur was the same color.

The widow lady had a special reason for giving the dogs their names. Kane was sometimes mean and he growled at anyone who came close to him. Able always wagged his tail when people came near, eager for a pat on his head or a scratch behind his ears.

Kane and Able played with the mother cat and kittens. The dogs would never hurt the kitties because they knew their mistress loved them. The five playmates were happy living at the tiny island cottage.

Early one morning Widow Lady was awakened by a *"Cock-a-doodle-doo! Cock-a-doodle-doo!"* She jumped out of bed and ran to the door.

Standing in the open doorway, she rubbed her eyes in disbelief. There, on the red ramp, perched a white rooster—the most beautiful rooster she had ever seen. His long tail feathers stood tall and proud.

The widow lady knew this was no ordinary rooster. She went back inside and pulled a big book from her bookshelf.

This was no ordinary book. It had facts about almost anything in the world anybody wanted to know about.

Lo and behold! Twenty roosters filled one entire page. Each rooster had a red crown on top of its head. But only one was covered in white feathers. This was a leghorn rooster.

For the next three weeks Widow Lady and the cats and dogs were awakened early each morning by *"Cock-a-doodle-doo!"* The leghorn also crowed during the afternoon, wandering all around the yard. Widow Lady chased the rooster and tried to shoo him away. She chased around and around the tiny cottage, but he would not leave.

After all the running, Widow Lady grew very tired. She knew the beautiful leghorn rooster had made himself at home.

Deep down, she was pleased he stayed. He was *ssssoooooo* beautiful!

"What shall I name this rooster?" she asked herself.

The following morning about five o'clock Widow Lady awoke to the leghorn's *"Cock-a-doodle-doo!"* She had watched him during afternoons as he strutted around the yard, crowing. He moved about with a skip or a hop, boastful with his high steps. He probably had a high opinion of himself.

His crowing and strutting had a special rhythm—like the music of Wolfgang Amadeus Mozart, a great classical composer who lived in the 1700s. If the rooster was going to stay, Widow Lady decided, she would call him Amadeus.

Amadeus wasted no time letting the other animals know he was boss of the yard.

He flew up into an old live oak tree. Perched on a dark limb, he had a great view of the field below, with its thousands of colorful wildflowers. From atop the oak, he could also survey the yard around the tiny cottage and see what the cats and dogs were doing. He decided to make his bed in that tree.

Around dawn each day, Amadeus announced to Widow Lady, Kane, Able, Mae Liza, Scooter, and Pumpkin that he was awake. In fact, his *"Cock-a-doodle-doo!"* was heard throughout the small Corners community of St. Helena.

Watching Amadeus strut and peck around the yard gave the widow lady much pleasure. She threw out corn for him to eat, but he was picky and would not eat it. One day she tossed a stale Kaiser roll outside. To her surprise, Amadeus pecked away at it. "How outrageous!" she thought. But every week, on her trip to the supermarket, she bought Kaiser rolls just for her beautiful leghorn rooster.

Amadeus annoyed Scooter and Pumpkin, waking them so early in the morning. The kittens rubbed their eyes with their little paws and complained, "Why does he have to wake us so early? We don't get any sleep anymore."

Cuddling her kittens, Mae Liza gave them their morning baths. "Oh dear, oh dear," she thought, "our mistress has given Amadeus too much freedom around here."

Amadeus loved to perch on the railing of the red ramp and *"Cock-a-doodle-doo!"* It didn't matter whether it was morning or afternoon.

Visitors came from near and far to see Amadeus. A minister from Romania, a small East European country, and a minister from Kansas City, Missouri, came. How delighted they were to see such a majestic rooster. He was a favorite of all the children in the community.

One day the widow lady was in the wash room of her tiny cottage when she heard a knock at the door. "Just a minute," she said. "I'll be right there."

The visitor knocked again . . . and again. The knocking grew louder.

Walking toward the door, Widow Lady called, "Just a minute, please."

She pulled open the door and there stood Amadeus. The widow lady threw her head back and laughed. She laughed so hard tears ran down her cheeks.

Amadeus perched on the railing of the red ramp and began to *"Cock-a-doodle-doo"* as loudly as he could.

Scooter and Pumpkin witnessed the whole scene. Their mistress sure did love the new rooster! "Does this mean Amadeus is the widow lady's favorite?" they wondered.

The kittens and mother cat huddled together on the north side of the yard. They were very displeased.

"We've got to get rid of Amadeus," Mae Liza exclaimed. "Just look at him all puffed up! Now our mistress no longer loves us, but she adores him."

The three began to hatch a plan. "Here's how it will work," explained the mother cat. "We will scratch and scratch to start a hole where the dogs are chained. Kane and Able can pull loose from the post and chase Amadeus away."

The kittens and mother cat knew Kane and Able were suspected of killing neighborhood chickens. Everybody on St. Helena talked about it. But the widow lady would not listen to that kind of talk. "I never listen to that kind of talk," she said.

Widow Lady did not leave her dogs chained all the time. Every day she leashed Kane and Able and took them on a three-and-a-half-mile walk to and from the St. Helena post office. Residents watched and waved as the three walked by.

Early one morning, to the cats' delight, Kane and Able pulled themselves loose. Widow Lady was surprised to see the dogs run past her window. Looking out, she watched in horror as the dogs raced about, each holding a chicken in his mouth. She called to them, but they paid her no attention. Anyway, it was too late. The chickens were already dead. The dogs settled down under a shade tree, proud of their catch. They did not know they had done anything wrong.

The widow lady fell into deep despair. She held her head in her hands and wept. She felt sad for the poor chickens. But she knew if Kane and Able would kill the neighbors' chickens, they might also kill Amadeus.

Feeling she had no choice, Widow Lady called the animal shelter and asked them to take the dogs away. "Maybe," she said, "someone will have a large fenced yard where they can play and stay out of trouble."

Scooter, Pumpkin, and Mae Liza were very sad. Their friends were gone and Amadeus was still there. If Widow Lady got rid of Kane and Able, they decided, she might also get rid of them. "She doesn't love us anymore," Mae Liza moaned. "And Amadeus is the boss of the yard. We must leave too."

After the kittens and mother cat left, Amadeus became lonely. He liked them and thought of the kittens as his playmates. Oftentimes people passing by the tiny cottage saw Amadeus pinning Mae Liza down with his feet on her back so she could not cuddle and play with her kittens. Amadeus thought Scooter and Pumpkin belonged to him.

Weeks passed. Amadeus spent his days wandering around the yard. His *"Cock-a-doodle-doo"* began to sound weak and he grew frail. He was so unhappy.

Widow Lady was sad too. Her little cottage had once been so joyful. One evening at dusk she looked up in the tall dark oak tree to wish good night to Amadeus. But Amadeus was not there.

Days went by and Amadeus did not return. The widow lady began telling her friends that her prized rooster was missing. Her heart was broken.

Amadeus had left as suddenly as he appeared.

Today, the widow lady still lives in her tiny cottage. She misses her animal friends and remembers when her yard was filled with activity and play. To all who will listen, Widow Lady tells the tale of Amadeus, the amazing white rooster.

Dear Reader,

I've written this story down so that you too can know about Amadeus, the leghorn rooster of St. Helena Island. If you visit the South Carolina coast, please keep an eye out for him. Perhaps he went to live with Scooter and Pumpkin in their new home. Wherever he is, I hope he is happy.

Delores B. Nevils

Dedicated to

Annella
Marsha, Bob, Gerald, and Linda
The Braswell Family
My only sister, Gladys Haynes
My brothers, Bill and John, and my grandchildren

Acknowledgements

I'd like to acknowledge the support, assistance, and encouragement of the following: The Arts Council of Beaufort County, South Carolina; Jonathan Green who loved my story and illustrated it with such brilliance; Amanda Gallman, Sandlapper Publishing Co., Inc., my publisher; Barbara Stone, my editor; Christine L. Stanley, Bay Street Trading Company, Beaufort; Pam Coaxum, St. Helena Island, who inspired me to write the story; Mildred Warren, New York, who insisted I get the story published; Marie Ferguson, who cared for Amadeus when I was out of town; Natalie Daise, Miss Natalie's Workshop; Lynn Corliss, Brad Burnham, and Janet Dolly Nash, my strong supporters; Tommy L. Williams, Slidell, LA, who had faith in my book; the University of South Carolina at Beaufort, for allowing me into the classroom to read my story; Marge Jarvis, Dataw Island, for inviting me to read the story of Amadeus at St.Helena Elementary School to first graders who loved it and asked poignant questions; Ellen Zisholz, Alluette Jones Smalls, Susan Madison, and Jan Spencer, all of whom assisted me in many ways; George D. Kessler, regional coordinator, Master Tree Farmer, Clemson Extension Service, for 2004; and the many unnamed folks of Beaufort County and elsewhere who gave me encouragement and moral support.

ABOUT THE AUTHOR:

Delores B. Nevils was born in Tewksbury, Massachusets. When she was six months old she went to live with her grandparents on the Ogeeche River in Davisboro, Georgia, where she became rooted in the Geeche culture. At age seven she moved to New York City. She attended Washington Irving High School and Manhattan Community College. She received a scholarship from Cooper Union Fine Arts School and was a member of the Art League in Manhattan.

Nevils moved to the Low Country of South Carolina in 1977. Here, her creative juices have flowed. She has worked as a sign painter, a contributor to the local newspaper, and a master tree farmer for Clemson University's Cooperative Extension Service, Southern Region. She is a member of the Penn Club at Penn Center on St. Helena Island, as well as the advisory council of Brainerd Heritage Project, Chester, South Carolina. She is one of two incorporators of the Gullah Festival of South Carolina. Her hobbies include photography, horseback riding, cooking, and singing. When movie companies film in the Beaufort area, she sometimes enjoys playing an "extra."

Nevils met Jonathan Green in 1989. Sharing a deep interest in the arts and local history, they became fast friends and remain close today. *Amadeus* is their first collaboration.

photo by Charles Allen Smith
© 2004

ABOUT THE ARTIST:

Noted art critics and reviewers consider Jonathan Green one of the most important painters of the southern experience. His work, which has been exhibited in major venues nationally and internationally, reflects an intrinsic sense of history and place. He first found support for his interest in the arts at Beaufort High School, near Gardens Corner, South Carolina, where he was born and raised. He left the state to study at the School of the Art Institute in Chicago, where he received a bachelor of fine arts degree.

Green's paintings chronicle the vibrant lives of his extended family and neighbors from the rural African American community of his childhood. Tales and rituals passed down orally for generations are now immortalized visually through his interpretive, colorful adaptations. A monograph published by McKissick Museum in Columbia, South Carolina, declares, ". . . his paintings appear pure, innocent, and honest. He pulls the past generations to the present and builds a bridge between the two. In the process he emphasizes the importance of love, belonging, and a sense of spirituality and work."

Recognizing Green's outstanding and extensive documentation of southern culture and traditions, the University of South Carolina awarded him in 1996 an honorary doctorate in fine art.

Jonathan Green has previously published *Gullah Images: The Art of Jonathan Green* [University of South Carolina Press, 1996].

FIRST EDITION

Published by Sandlapper Publishing Co., Inc.
Orangeburg, South Carolina 29115

Printed in Korea

Each illustration in this book is an oil painting, which was photo-
graphed for transparency, scanned by laser, and then reproduced in
full color. Photos of the paintings were taken by Tim Stamm.

Library of Congress Cataloging-in-Publication Data

Nevils, Delores B., 1932–
    Amadeus, the leghorn rooster / story by Delores B. Nevils ;
illustrations by Jonathan Green.— 1st ed.
        p. cm.
    Summary: Widow Lady is very happy in her island cottage with her
family of cats and dogs until a rooster appears and decides that he is boss
of the yard.
    ISBN 0-87844-174-3 (hardcover : alk. paper)
    [1. Roosters—Fiction. 2. Dogs—Fiction. 3. Cats—Fiction. 4. Saint
Helena Island (S.C.)—Fiction.] I. Green, Jonathan, 1955– ill. II.
Title.

PZ7.N4652Am 2004
[E]—dc22
                                                                2004010153